PARAZIM

Strong   Warrior   Woman

This Guidebook belongs to:

 _____

a powerful warrior.

ISBN 10: 1543007325

ISBN-13: 978-1543007329

PARAZIM

Strong Warrior Woman

The Author is a U.S. Army Veteran, Fear Factor Contestant,
and Silicon Valley Lawyer. She is the Recipient of The Army
Achievement Medal for International Journalism and
The Witkin Award for Gender and the Law.

HARMONY OSWALD, ESQ.

PARAZIM, Strong Warrior Woman is dedicated to all of the brave warriors of the past, present, and future including Sterling, Mom, Linda, Gram W., Gram I., Nunny, Wendy, Kelly, Nisha, Mary Ann, Mil, Apryle, Natalie, Jessica, Cassie, Mandy, Rylen, Brooklyn, Londyn, Ava, Mercy, Grace, Kirsten, Natalia, Anita, Alison, Stephanie, Laura, Ellie, PJ, and the list goes on...

May positive energy be with you always, shining light and love upon your individual path to breakthrough.

Strong warrior women are bold and powerful.

When sisters join forces in unity,

thunderous breakthroughs occur.

Breakthrough Habitude

In past times, men worked outside of the home while women supported them behind the scenes. In the workforce, men lifted each other up like a band of brothers.

Today, the strong warrior woman, like many females, invests in her own career. When new opportunities arise around her, she looks for ways to help her fellow woman succeed. She respects and honors the sanctity of the sisterhood. The warrior wisely recognizes that when sisters join forces in unity, thunderous breakthroughs occur.

WWI (Women's World #1)

"Come along, GIRLS!" she exclaims to the group of men standing before her. Smirks and confusion fill the air. The strong warrior woman aptly notes that on a daily basis, people refer to females as guys. "Thanks, guys!" or "How's it going, guys?" are phrases commonly heard and accepted by women in society. Yet, when males are referred to as "girls," they largely renounce the label due to implicit bias toward characteristics traditionally labeled as feminine. The warrior reveals to the group before her that men should be grateful and proud to be referred to as "women" or "girls." After all, females are strong, bold, and powerful.

Pick Your Platoon

Time is a limited resource. For this reason, the strong warrior woman is particular about with whom she shares the journey. In the past, there were moments when she gave away her energy to individuals who did not appreciate or deserve her attention. With this experience, she learned a useful lesson, and she will not make the same mistake again. Before going into battle, the strong warrior woman exercises great care in choosing her companions. She eliminates toxic people from her inner circle. She only shares the gift of her time with those who believe in her and support her mission. The warrior picks her platoon.

Spotlight On Wellness

"I'm feeling under the weather" is a phrase sometimes offered as an excuse to take a leave of absence from the battlefield. The strong warrior woman is highly dedicated to her mission and recognizes that good health is vital to her success. She purposefully cares for her body, mind, and spirit. Her actions help her to maintain the harmonious balance of positive energies necessary to fight the good fight. She refuses to dwell upon thoughts of illness. She consistently envisions good health and wellness. The warrior is strong, bold, and powerful. She will rise up and conquer the day!

HARMONY OSWALD, ESQUIRE

Dream And Do

It is does not require a tremendous amount of effort to speak fancy rhetoric. The strong warrior woman knows that merely talking about what could or should be done is insufficient. She must arouse mighty courage from within her to take the plunge and begin what is in her heart. With strength, conviction, and a momentous leap of faith, she embarks on her journey. She perseveres with unwavering dedication. The act of getting started and following through until the end sets apart the dreamers from the achievers. The warrior receives heavy favor from the universe as she works to fulfill her mission.

Daily Celebrations

When the warrior feels bored, she contemplates what she can do to change this. She recognizes that deep within her is the power to transform any ordinary, lackluster day into a festive, special occasion. While the boring remain bored, she embraces every opportunity to live life to the fullest. She knows that with the right perspective, she can transform a mundane task into something vibrant, colorful, and exciting. She perceives life as a gift and a joyous miracle. The strong warrior woman approaches each new day with jubilant celebration.

HARMONY OSWALD, ESQUIRE

Introduction To Heroes

The strong warrior woman travels along the path meeting countless extraordinary and talented women who greatly influence her journey. She makes every effort to live in a constant state of mindfulness, where she remains present and alert to witness the magic of the meeting. She understands that each human soul has a special gift for those who are prepared to accept it. She opens her heart and mind in anticipation of whatever the universe might offer her. When the moon shines bright and the stars align, the warrior meets a hero.

Break The Roles

Good girls are taught to follow societal "roles" for appropriate behaviors. Often these guidelines create harmful limitations and result in unconscious bias toward women who do not fit the mold. The strong warrior woman refuses to accept preconceived notions about who or what she should be. She recognizes that stereotypes associated with gender, race, age, and more prevent people from fully contributing their individual gifts and talents to the world. She views limits placed upon women like her as an invitation to breakthrough. She boldly moves forward with her mission. The warrior has a destiny to fulfill.

Mind Your Business

The warrior notices that some people dedicate their entire lives to critiquing others. These people make excellent teachers. As she watches them attempting to control the world, she becomes keenly aware that it is not her place to act as judge. At times, her mind suggests that she too possesses the authority to evaluate "lesser capable" souls. When this occurs, the warrior remains still and observes this thought, recognizing it as a distortion of the truth. She rightfully surrenders the duty of judgment to the universe. The warrior is busy pursuing her own personal legend. She has no desire to also take on the role of God.

Aim High

Thinking small is safe and easy. A person can simply look at what other people traditionally do and then copy to get similar results. The strong warrior woman takes the path less traveled. She views life as an amazing gift and a grand opportunity. She has lofty goals and dreams of making a positive difference in the world. She is committed to her own originality, even if others don't always understand her at first. Because she believes she can accomplish something extraordinary, the universe helps the warrior to breakthrough.

Accept What Is

From time to time, the strong warrior woman crosses the path of a person who becomes angry, disheartened, or frustrated. When this occurs, she remains grounded and alert in order to accept strong emotions in others who are on a journey of their own. She recognizes that she can naturally and reasonably only control her own thoughts and actions. She calmly addresses the situation with empathy, compassion, and acceptance while maintaining external boundaries. She shields herself from negative emotions displayed by others. At day's end, the undaunted warrior stands peaceful, focused, and strong.

Law of Thinkspeak

Every thought pondered and every word spoken commingles with the universe to create the warrior's present state of reality. Fortunately, she is acutely aware that within this truth lies immense power. She applies this principle with the highest level of quality and care. She thinks honorable and magnificent thoughts and delivers her words with utmost intention and purpose. Her desires merge with the heavens and the stars align to help her. She gains supernatural guidance and favor from the universe. The strong warrior woman is connected to a force and mission that is greater than her own.

HARMONY OSWALD, ESQUIRE

Guideposts

The strong warrior woman accepts matters she cannot change and takes action in areas of her life where she does possess power to influence the results. She notices that certain engagements cause her to feel amazing. Unsurprisingly, these circumstances create a bounce in her step and a twinkle in her eye. When possible, she spends her valuable time with people and in activities that elevate her state of mind and leave her feeling fabulous. She stays alert and makes wise decisions. As a result, the warrior shines like the sun!

Do You

The warrior knows herself best. She is aware of her chief attributes and commits to developing them. She identifies one trait that distinguishes her, and she focuses on sharpening her skills in that area. Sometimes people offer free advice, saying, "This is what successful people do. If you want to be successful, do this!" The warrior is not tempted by this flawed instruction. She knows that truly successful people embrace authenticity and share their unique gifts with the world. The strong warrior woman feels at home and empowered, because she persists in following her individual path to breakthrough.

Let Go And Go

Don't look back! Holding on to the past only inhibits progress. The strong warrior woman understands the value of letting go in order to make room for a fresh new chapter in the book of life. Nothing in this world is worth the heavy weight and setbacks caused by holding on to the mistakes or regrets of yesteryear. The warrior performs an about face. With great courage, she releases what is behind and looks with anticipation toward what's in store for her future. She boldly marches forward in the direction of a bright new day. Up the road, around the bend, and just beyond the horizon, a breakthrough awaits her.

Focus On The Goal

The many distractions of modern life such as social media, technology, products, and events can quickly lead a warrior down a long and winding side road. The strong warrior woman knows that each day is a gift to embrace, and she must stay on track in order to complete her mission. With this in mind, she focuses intently on her goal, seeking it out with the fierce dedication and determination of a soldier on a mission. She establishes her priorities and removes all frivolous distractions from her arena. She is highly committed to fulfilling her purpose. The warrior keeps her eye on the prize.

HARMONY OSWALD, ESQUIRE

Walls of Protection

Sometimes a spirit of negativity surrounds a person so completely that any amount of time in their presence will drag even the most resilient warrior down to the pits of the abyss. The strong warrior woman is on a mission. She realizes that repeated recovery from a life depleting force is not helpful to her journey. She carefully chooses her companions and bravely establishes and maintains healthy boundaries to keep toxic energy and people out of her life. She has battles to wage and wars to win. Protective walls create a safe haven so the warrior can focus on more pressing matters, like forging a path to breakthrough.

Embrace The Void

There are times when every warrior experiences the urge to explain. In these moments, she instead chooses to allow silence to work on her behalf. She is peaceful and still because she realizes it is not necessary to state every detail of her plan. She knows what she is doing, and she trusts in her own leadership abilities. Wise warriors of the past once revealed that it is acceptable and sometimes even advisable to remain a mystery. The strong warrior woman embraces her quiet space and exploits it for higher purposes. She leaves some of the details out, providing room for the imagination of the universe to explore.

Enshrine Promises

The sanctity of a promise should be consistently honored. With utmost respect and full appreciation for this principle, the strong warrior woman gives her word. Then, she reveres it as a sacred vow. Peers sharing the journey view a promise from her as valuable chattel equivalent to silver or gold. The people around her know well that they can trust her to under-promise and over-perform. Her reputation in the community is stellar. She is viewed as a reliable source and a dedicated leader. The warrior is a woman of her word.

Steadfast Generosity

The strong warrior woman is independent and self-reliant. Although she believes in the power of teamwork and understands that big visions require the collaboration of many, she also holds a secret. Underneath the shiny armor is a steadfast soul capable of powerful movements. With this truth in her heart, she gives to her fellow woman much more than she takes. She spreads goodness with an open heart and reflective mind; never out of mandate, guilt, or fear. In return, the universe favors the warrior and showers her with abundance both in love and in life.

Natural Allies

No matter how phenomenal the warrior, not everyone will be cheering for her day of triumph. The strong warrior woman does not pay much attention to a "Negative Nate" or a simple critic with ill intentions. She understands the benefit of focusing on inspirational thoughts and positive people. At times when it feels like she is left alone on the battlefield, she envisions the army of fellow warriors who went before her. Within a gentle breeze or a sunbeam, she feels encouragement and support uplifting her. The warrior knows that many important battles are won in the constructs of the mind.

Humble Virtues

Pretentious soldiers provoke war. The strong warrior woman understands that everyone is different, and no particular path or warrior is better than another. She applies her own gifts and talents to fight the good fight. She respects her companions who use their own abilities to fight a battle different than hers. She does not willfully offend, inspire jealousy, or incite violence in the hearts of others. Every one of her endeavors is accomplished in a quiet, humble manner. She does not need to prove superiority in order to believe in the value of her mission. The way of the warrior is grounded, confident, and secure.

Mind Control

The external realities of the universe are birthed inside the intricacies of the mind. The strong warrior woman knows it is important to keep this hardworking computer in check. Meditation helps to ensure her brain does not partake in excessive, uncontrolled thinking. She engages her mind to solve problems with specific clarity of purpose. She develops goals, evaluates strategies, analyzes problems, and reviews solutions. Then, with peace and confidence, she moves forward with her mission. The warrior uses her mind as a helpful tool when needed. She never allows her mind to control her.

Forget Critics

Many people would rather face death than publicly perform. Upon taking the stage of life, the strong warrior woman stays centered, maintaining full awareness that her mission involves giving gifts, not collecting reviews. Negative critics may arise but will never triumph over her, because she makes a positive impact on the world. When she presents before an audience, she does so in love, peace, and with complete abandon of self-centered thoughts. Her performance exudes truth, beauty, and raw authenticity. Her gift is not always perfect but in keeping it real, the warrior holds the power to change the world.

One Revolutionary Idea

Some people conjure up so many ideas that listening to them speak is enough to make a person's head spin. The strong warrior woman believes that innovation is vital but one timely and useful idea is all it takes to positively impact the world. She becomes highly knowledgeable in her field and develops a keen awareness of related societal issues. She develops useful solutions and prepares to act when the moment is right. Critics jeer, "She has no plan! She is wasting her time!" Then, with all the punctuality and poise of a woman on a mission, the warrior triumphantly breaks through.

Look Fear In The Eye

The warrior is not fearless. There are days when she feels very afraid, alone, and vulnerable. She begins to think she will never get ahead. During these times, she summons all of the courage and determination she can muster to face her fears and overcome the challenges ahead. The difference between the average Jane and the strong warrior woman is in her response to perceived danger. The warrior never allows fear to deter her. She is always certain to do the thing she is most afraid to do. The warrior is not fearless, but she is strikingly bold and shockingly brave.

HARMONY OSWALD, ESQUIRE

Believe In Miracles

When waiting for an answer, expect a "yes." The strong warrior woman knows that worrying never helps her to accomplish anything worthwhile. For this reason, she allows herself the freedom to imagine that a wondrous miracle is about to occur. This allows positive energy to flow abundantly throughout her life and gives the universe permission to work magic on her behalf. Nothing is lost and everything is gained by moving forward believing in the power of possibilities. As the warrior makes her way along the path, good fortune awaits her just beyond the horizon.

Stealth Training

No one likes a show-off. The strong warrior woman is clever and strong, but she is careful not to flaunt her talents with a goal of impressing others. She is confident enough in her own abilities that she does not feel the need to gain outward approval. She privately accumulates amazing knowledge and reliable experience that will help her when the day of battle arrives. People say, "Things are so easy for her. She is one of the luckies!" She smiles and accepts the compliment. The warrior trains hard, and she views remarks like this as rewards from the universe for fighting the good fight.

HARMONY OSWALD, ESQUIRE

Foolproof Management

A fool thinks too little and talks too much. The strong warrior woman recognizes this trap when it appears before her. She knows if she engages with an unreasonable person, she will soon also begin to appear as a buffoon. With all of the patience she can muster, she quietly observes the speaker... and a miracle occurs! The person talking becomes discontent with her lack of response. The warrior breathes a sigh of relief as the one-way conversation dissipates. The world returns to business as usual.

Powerful Persistence

When working toward an important goal becomes extremely difficult, it is a sign that the desired outcome is quite valuable. The warrior understands that there are no shortcuts to greatness. Perseverance through tough times is the sole element separating the common majority from those fighting the good fight. Blood, sweat, and tears build strength, stamina, and character. It is often the champion of the most treacherous battle who ultimately wins the war. The strong warrior woman pushes through, even when things become much tougher than expected.

Pathfinder

Expressing misery and resentment regarding current circumstances is a way of life for some people. They feel helpless and angry because their story did not turn out as they had hoped. The strong warrior woman knows that the present moment is a direct result of the thoughts and choices she made in the past. She understands that in order to have the life she always dreamed of, she must be clear about her desires and communicate them to the universe through her thoughts and words today. With great purpose, she makes high quality decisions. What the warrior selects in this moment is precisely what the warrior receives.

Travel Lightly

A wise owl once reported that eagles soar because they move with grace, assurance, and take themselves lightly. In much the same way, the warrior's confidence and willingness to laugh at her perceived flaws is beneficial. The heavy weight associated with maintaining perfection ultimately leads to failure. When critical self-judgment creeps in, the warrior casts the idea in a humorous light. If she thinks someone dislikes her, she brushes it off, labeling it the "Who Hates Me Now" theory. The moment she laughs, all negativity dissolves. The strong warrior woman soars through life because she takes herself lightly.

HARMONY OSWALD, ESQUIRE

Sacrificial Exposure

The warrior volunteers to engage at the front lines of battle. This choice leaves her fully exposed to the elements. Enemy combatants can easily view the moves she is making. There are plenty of times when critics embrace the opportunity to evaluate her tactics. She does not allow this to hinder her progress. She stands firm because she is confident with her own decision-making and ability to breakthrough. The strong warrior woman knows that vulnerability and exposure are some of the sacrifices she must make to arrive at victory.

Refresh

She works hard. People count on her. Life gets busy. The strong warrior woman begins to feel that she has no personal time for herself. When this occurs, she recognizes the need to set aside a day for health and wellness. She takes a paid personal day or an unpaid day off to enjoy life and simply relax. In the long run, she knows that days of rest and still reflection provide her body and mind with refreshing renewal. This helps her to return to the fray re-energized to fight the good fight with the strength and audacity of a mighty warrior.

Love Love

The strong warrior woman recognizes that the universe will undoubtedly shoot the deeds of her life back at her with accurate precision. Remembering this universal law, she works hard to fulfill her purpose while never losing sight of what matters most. She cares deeply for her family and friends, serves her community, and does her best to act with kindness and empathy toward her fellow woman. The warrior keeps in mind that when opportunities to show compassion and love are lost forever in the heat of battle, ultimately nobody wins the war.

Dissolve Expectations

Some people go through life constantly disappointed by the actions of those around them. They cannot understand why certain individuals continuously fail to meet the standards of acceptable behaviors they personally developed. The strong warrior woman recognizes that holding others to rigid specifications and feeling continuously offended when they fail to adequately meet them is a waste of her valuable time and energy. She is on a mission and has an important duty to fulfill. The wise warrior focuses upon items within her scope of control.

HARMONY OSWALD, ESQUIRE

"U" In Adventure

As the old adage goes, a person who is bored is probably simply a bore. The strong warrior woman never settles for anything less than fabulous. She seeks out the best life has to offer. She surrounds herself with people and circumstances that create a gleam in her eye and a bounce in her step. She is the essence and life of the party. In fact, the celebration starts the moment she walks in the front door. "She is a superstar!" people comment as she makes her way across the room. People admire the warrior because she represents the human embodiment of adventure.

Active Duty

At times, people express themselves indirectly, weaving in and out and all around the facts to a degree that causes others to miss the point. The strong warrior woman notices this human tendency and therefore purposefully engages in active listening with an open heart and mind. She hears not only to gather the information stated but also to comprehend what is actually meant. In the end, if she remains unclear, she asks thoughtful questions to better understand the speaker before her. The warrior recognizes that clear communication is a key element to success.

Fluid Necessity

As the strong warrior woman continues to bravely fight the good fight in hopes of realizing her dream, she begins to encounter obstacles in her way. Progress is slow and painful, and the path is not as pleasant as she had imagined. At such times, she takes on the characteristics of water. She flows out and around large boulders in her path while continuing to move in the direction of the sea. The warrior recognizes that accomplishing any worthwhile goal requires moving with the flow, while pushing forward with tremendous power and persistence.

Equal Opportunity

Historically, women supported men in the workforce. Men were systematically touted as "successful" and celebrated for their accomplishments, while women were rarely recognized for their contributions to upholding the social structure. The strong warrior woman refuses to give up her dream so a partner can live theirs. She understands that healthy relationships involve mutual honor and support for the goals and aspirations of the other. When the warrior chooses to take part in a relationship, it involves reciprocal cooperation and cost sharing, and results in a win/win outcome for both parties.

HARMONY OSWALD, ESQUIRE

Make It Count

Working to pick up a paycheck on Friday is a common survival tactic. The warrior believes there is more to life than merely going through the motions to exist. She takes the time necessary to learn about the society she lives in and the people who are fighting the good fight on the battlefield next to her. She listens intently with a goal of understanding the world's problems. Once she arrives at the one idea for which she can live and die, she follows her heart with all the power and persistence of a woman on a mission. She understands her duty. The warrior's purpose is to positively impact the world.

In Command

Power can never be stolen. It can only be freely given away. The strong warrior woman stays strong and centered, in spite of naysayers who try to influence her decision making to meet their own goals. She does not give other people permission to hold her back from her destiny. She knows where she is headed and what she is capable of. She marches along the path she chose with confidence and conviction. She accepts feedback and makes changes when she decides it will improve her strategy. The warrior is independent, and her life is her own.

HARMONY OSWALD, ESQUIRE

Self-Investment

Much to do in limited time - such is the dilemma of life. The strong warrior woman understands that each moment is valuable. She remains keenly aware of the type of activities she partakes in. She notices that some actions such as helping a mentee, exercising, or reading a good book, strengthen her inner warrior. Other items, such as worrying or watching news, tend to suck the lifeblood right out of her, leaving her weak and weary. With purposeful calculation, she engages in activities that motivate her heart and energize her soul. Seasons may change, but time remains an ally of the warrior.

Prolific Innovation

The best problem solvers are creative thinkers. The strong warrior woman views life as a blank canvas. She does not strictly look to tradition or jump to conclusions based on how other people see things. She does not accept that there is only one way of reaching a desired outcome or that certain things simply cannot be done. She was provided with a sharp mind and a strong spirit. She shares her gifts and talents like a billionaire set on going broke. The universe moves mountains to help her succeed. Creative ingenuity drives the warrior to greatness.

Heart Of A Warrior

Society regularly obsesses over outward appearances. As a result, many people travel along the path completely unaware that the most effective beauty product is living a life filled with peace, love, and kindness. The strong warrior woman has a heart filled with gorgeous love that radiates positive energy into the far depths of the universe. Her beautiful, grounded character and strong, mindful spirit shine brightly, like sunlight beaming from the heavens. When a boot fits, she proudly wears it, and Sterling Heart is her battle name.

Insights

Meanwhile, the rock we endearingly call home continues to spiral on its axis through space. Life on Earth is a mystery. The strong warrior woman does not hold the key to unlock a door revealing all secrets of the universe. Therefore, she does not judge others who offer philosophies or opinions that differ from her own. As she faithfully rides the planet, she continues to learn and grow. With an open heart, she gives thanks to her fellow woman for the insights, wisdom, and other gifts so graciously shared along the way. The warrior is grateful for the journey.

Lighten The Load

Holding a grudge against a perceived transgressor is a heavy burden for the strongest warrior to drag into battle. When there is no one else to blame because she herself has erred, failing to forgive takes an even heftier toll. The strong warrior woman recognizes the limits of humanity. She avoids perfectionism and instead seeks excellence in herself and others. When mistakes arise, she asks others to forgive her, and she quickly forgives her companion's faults as well. The warrior travels lightly, and her soul is filled with peace as she makes her way toward her destination.

Success Is Now

Striving for a day when success is finally achieved is a common endeavor. People imagine that after many years of toil, the future will reveal a season filled with personal contentment, respect, and admiration from peers. The strong warrior woman recognizes that always looking to the future without maintaining a present state of awareness is unwise. Today is a gift. Tomorrow is never guaranteed. With this in mind, she approaches each new day as an opportunity to live a life filled with purpose and love. She is grateful for how far she has come on her journey. Progress is the prize. The warrior is successful today.

Tenets Of Battle

Peer pressure and groupthink tend to heavily influence the weak and timid. The strong warrior woman understands her own mission and knows the specific actions she will take to succeed. She is clear about what she will and will not do, and she is firm about what she does and does not stand for. Because of her steady moral compass, she is able to function in a world filled with chaos, uncertainty, and pressure with a high level of strength, determination, and consistency. The warrior's principles are tested and true.

Purple Comets

Deep within the whimsical heart of a child lies the ability to dream and fantasize about everyday miracles. Only certain remarkable people carry this gift into adulthood. The strong warrior woman is aware of her superpower. Her journey is filled with hope, love, and a commitment to helping her fellow woman. She joins forces with the universe, approaching each new day with courage and resolve to cross oceans and move mountains. She believes in the magic of utopia and dreams. The warrior beholds a robust vision and it compels her to breakthrough.

HARMONY OSWALD, ESQUIRE

Leaders Act

The shrill echo of an angry commander's tone can dishearten even the most resilient and cooperative soldier. The strong warrior woman understands it is not what is said, but how it is said that often makes a difference. When she feels annoyed, she takes the time necessary to regain a sense of control over this emotion. Once she is calm, she addresses the situation with purpose and clarity of thought. She delivers her message firmly, with a warm and pleasant demeanor. People respond positively to her style of conflict resolution. Out of respect and gratitude toward the warrior, her students go out of their way to help her.

Mystery Of The Ages

Due to media driven age bias in modern culture, many women wish that they could remain forever young. Rather than appreciating getting better, they mourn getting older. The strong warrior woman feels comfortable and confident in her own skin. She does not conform to harmful stereotypes or unrealistic ideals. She celebrates lifelong progress and greets the future with excitement, a contagious smile, and a bit of hearty laughter. The warrior replaces girlish naivety with womanly poise, sophistication, mystery, and finesse.

Attention!

Some people do the same thing over and over again, in spite of being unhappy with the results. They never take a moment to reflect upon the expedience of an action or to consider how an adjustment might improve the outcome. The strong warrior woman takes a front row seat at the university of her life. She learns more and more, growing wise as the storyline progresses and the plot develops. Because she allows her life to teach her, she becomes fiercely sophisticated and phenomenally sharp in battle. In the school of warriors, she wins the award for "most improved."

Risk vs. Reward

Fear is a natural human prison that holds people back from living. When a person is so afraid of making a mistake that they refuse to take a chance and try something new, they never learn what they are truly capable of. The strong warrior woman makes it a habit to do what she has never done before. She understands that in doing so, she risks facing failure in her new endeavor. People say, "She always gets to do such amazing things!" The warrior nods in agreement. She does get to do amazing things, merely because she is not afraid to try.

Adjust The Sights

The warrior directly addresses difficulties that arise with both detachment and resolve. Depending on the circumstances, she makes a change, accepts the truth of the matter, or chooses to perceive the situation differently. If something is unacceptable to her, she analyzes the issue and attempts to make adjustments. If nothing can be done, she does not waste time dwelling on a perceived negative circumstance that she cannot control. She accepts what is or decides to think about it differently. The warrior chose her own path and never complains about the opportunity to fight the good fight.

Verbal Intelligence

In historic societies, males were taught to speak up and females were taught to sit in cooperative silence. The strong warrior woman finds flaws with both of these approaches. Wisdom resides not in always speaking or remaining silent but rather in finding balance. She knows she learns nothing while she talks. She views education as freedom. She learns about matters she cares about and practices speaking confidently in public forums. When she chooses to participate, she shares a valuable gift with the world. The warrior does not always speak, but when she does, people stop what they are doing to listen.

Uncomfortable Advantage

Comfort is the enemy of champions. The strong warrior woman views the absence of comfort as a sure sign that she is on target with fighting the good fight. Like anyone else, she cringes at struggle and detests the sweat dripping from her brow. She may not enjoy the pain, but she views hardships as small battles that are hers to win. She can either persevere in spite of challenges or toss in the white flag of surrender. Taking the easy road entices her briefly, but she decides to summon her inner courage and determination. The warrior embraces discomfort and rises to the occasion for a victory.

Dismiss The Petty, Officer

It is nearly impossible to overlook a drama king. Every small thing that goes wrong is catastrophic, and those around him should know and care. The warrior takes a different approach. She is on a mission, and she has a destiny to fulfill. Sometimes unusual circumstances arise. When this occurs, she takes note, makes adjustments if possible or necessary, and moves on. She is content in her life and does not need to dwell upon minor issues or put them on a pedestal for the world to see. The strong warrior woman appropriately differentiates between the miniscule and the big deal.

HARMONY OSWALD, ESQUIRE

Heavenly Sisterhood

When women compete with each other while men act as a band of brothers, women and girls lose every time. The strong warrior woman recognizes that females are strong, bold, and powerful. She believes women deserve to win! She supports her sisters every chance she gets. When she is offered a promotion or a breakthrough occurs in her career, she looks around for another female she can pull up the ladder with her. She understands the importance of honoring the sanctity of the sisterhood. Moreover, the warrior heard that there is a special place in heaven for women who help other women.

Avalanche

Society sometimes negatively judges people who continue to learn and grow, labeling them as "wanderers." Stereotypes demand that once people reach adulthood, they "settle down" and begin to act in a predictable manner. The strong warrior woman refuses to accept this limiting way of thinking. She values her right to develop and flourish in every stage of life. She realizes that as long as she keeps an open mind, she will continue to improve and progress. The wise warrior knows that rolling stones gain power and momentum as they move along the course.

VIP Assistance

When a person denies her own current state of reality, anxiety, depression, and relational issues begin to develop. The warrior refrains from judging particular situations as "good" or "bad." She aims to fully accept the entirety of the circumstance before her. She trusts that there are reasons why things occur that are beyond the scope of her own understanding. She does not feel the need to control nature. She has faith that in every situation, the universe will work things out in her favor. After all, she is a strong warrior woman.

Deliver Sandwiches

At times, constructive criticism can be helpful. For every critical comment, however, seven positive statements should be made. The goal is to inspire the masses. The warrior recognizes that people do not enjoy being negatively evaluated. For this reason, she picks her battles. When critical comment is necessary, she uses a sandwiching technique. She delivers the disapproving comment between two positive statements in order to soften the blow. She respects the dignity of her fellow woman. In doing so, the strong warrior woman honors herself.

Give The Order

Self-conscious thoughts sometimes inhibit an individual from asking for what they need or want. It is as if the person does not believe they deserve good things. Or worse, they don't think anyone will listen or take them seriously. The warrior recognizes that this type of behavior will get her nowhere. In order for the universe to understand where she is going, she must first be clear in her own mind and then communicate her desires and intentions with those around her. The strong warrior woman is bold and brave. She knows exactly what she wants, and she is not afraid to ask for it.

Warriors Can

Donny believes he cannot succeed. He is right! He exudes a losing attitude, and the universe agrees that he is a loser. The strong warrior woman refuses to think like a Downer Donny. She believes she is a winner. She is clear about her mission. She makes sacrifices and exercises self control. She perseveres in fighting the good fight. When people see her they say, "If anyone can do it, she is the one!" This is true. The warrior can do it, because she thinks she can.

HARMONY OSWALD, ESQUIRE

Smart Zipped

There is always that one person who has the quickest response and perfect answer. They easily maintain the spotlight on every occasion. The warrior remains purposefully alert, taking this all in. She is knowledgeable regarding issues of importance to her and is confident and capable of speaking when the moment is right. In selecting her words, she exercises precision and care. She regularly chooses to talk less in order to "be more." The strong warrior woman knows that people who never stop talking eventually say things they will later regret.

Principle Opponents

In modern society, people claim that "haters hate" and there is nothing anyone can do about it. The strong warrior woman knows that although it appears that some people are not her biggest fans, these individuals are not truly against her. The warrior has a heart of gold, and she is on a mission to positively impact the world. She approaches her day with gratitude and her companions with kindness. If someone opposes principles of goodness and truth, she does not take it personally. The universe raises up the warrior, so that she might deliver love to all of womankind.

Equipoise

Balance is a key component to any successful battle plan. The strong warrior woman knows that in order to effectively fight the good fight, she must properly maintain harmonious equipoise within her body, mind, and spirit. To achieve this, she grooms and cares for her body each day. She practices meditation and maintains a present state of awareness. She relaxes with people she loves and enjoys the peace and serenity of nature. Once balance is achieved, the warrior proceeds with confidence to complete her mission.

The Present Is Battle

People complain that labor is hard. The strong warrior woman recognizes that one of life's greatest gifts is the chance to work at an endeavor that she independently determined is worth spending her valuable time on. Life is extraordinary. The human condition provides the opportunity to feel, think, grow, and create. The warrior chooses her livelihood with purposeful calculation. Her work is a compilation of beautiful gifts shared with the universe. Her presents will resonate into eternity.

Warrior Woman

Due to stereotypes associated with the ideal male worker, women sometimes adjust their natural behaviors to conform to "masculine" norms at work. For example, a female might lower her voice, engage in social conversations regarding male-only sports, or otherwise act in ways to help her "fit in." The strong warrior woman knows that true equality exists only when a society also embraces and values characteristics traditionally labeled as "feminine." She aims for authenticity at all times. Tolerance, diversity, and inclusion are essential to progress, and the warrior unapologetically represents womankind.

Recharge

Social interaction is valuable and necessary, but striking a balance between public and private spheres of life is key to progress. The strong warrior woman notices that when she connects with the outer world via meetings, phone calls, and social media, after a while her attention becomes outwardly hyper-focused. If she is not careful, she begins to feel tired and manipulated. For this reason, she takes time regularly to unplug from public engagements. The warrior visits her inner space. Moments set aside for meditation and solitary reflection allow her to reconnect with the peace, serenity, and power necessary to fight the good fight.

HARMONY OSWALD, ESQUIRE

Right Face

Once there was a woman who strived only for power.
The universe noticed she lacked any care or concern
whatsoever for her fellow woman. No matter how hard she
tried, she could never breakthrough.

The warrior understands that to succeed in battle, she
must do the right thing, for the right reasons, for the right
period of time. The moment she releases all desire for
power, a transformation occurs. She becomes strong,
mighty, and more powerful than ever. The strong warrior
woman breaks through!

Stewardship Of The Greens

Money is not the root of all evil but greed and waste are. The strong warrior woman never judges a person negatively based on her fortune. She believes the more money a woman is blessed with, the more opportunity and responsibility she has to make a positive difference in the world. The warrior works hard, striving for financial freedom and independence. She focuses on being a good steward over her wealth. When a circumstance arises requiring her to choose between money and her companion, the choice is simple. The warrior firmly believes that humanity is more valuable than currency.

Strive For Excellence

Many of the world's greatest tragedies occur when a person seeks perfection rather than appreciating and celebrating excellence. The strong warrior woman recognizes that perfection is an ideal devised in the minds of fools. It is nothing more than a limiting stereotype that opposes and inhibits creative thought, ingenuity, and advancement. Brilliance and truth reside within the confines of perceived imperfections. The warrior strives for originality and excellence. When these qualities are present, she knows the atmosphere is ripe for breakthrough.

Corrective Action

The thought of making a mistake terrifies many people. The warrior knows this is a backward and very limiting way of thinking. Taking risks is necessary on the road to breakthrough. Failure is always a possibility where progress is sought. When defeat shows its ugly face, the warrior embraces the opportunity to learn a valuable lesson in fighting the good fight. During the next round, she will be smarter, stronger, and more capable of winning the battle. The warrior is alert and wise. She never makes the same mistake twice.

Delayed Gratification

In modern society, people expect instant gratification. Technology makes everything faster but also spawns impatient people who are unwilling to commit to long-term goals. The strong warrior woman is faced with two choices. She can settle for less and enjoy instant gratification. Alternatively, she can commit to behaviors that will pay off with much larger dividends in the future. She is committed to fulfilling her entire mission. The warrior exercises self-control so that she can eventually celebrate more than just a minor advantage. As a direct result of her choice to delay gratification, the warrior claims a major victory.

Battle Dance

Breaking down a door to force an immediate entry is usually not the best plan of action. The strong warrior woman fully trusts in the timing and seasons of nature. She prepares herself now so that when a pathway opens up, she is ready for action. She recognizes that if she misses an opportunity, it may never come again. She patiently waits and observes, then moves forward with calculated purpose, and eventually engages her exit strategy, all in due time. The battle dance of the warrior flows naturally with the rhythm of life.

Path To Greatness

As the warrior travels and meets people along the way, she learns of shortcuts. If she turns right, she can save a few miles. If she turns left, she can avoid a blocked roadway. The warrior remembers that the goal of her voyage is to visit new lands and to collect souvenirs from the journey. The road itself will teach and guide her. She could take an alternative route to reach her destination more quickly, but in doing so, she will arrive unfulfilled and empty handed. The warrior decides to stick to her designated path. There are no shortcuts to where she is going.

Overflow Your Canteen

When a warrior searches outside of herself for personal gratification and contentment, she becomes stuck in a never-ending cycle of disappointment. The strong warrior woman knows that she alone is responsible for satisfying her inner craving for acceptance and love. With mindful awareness and clarity of purpose, she engages in daily acts of self-compassion, care, and kindness. Her heart becomes filled to the brim with joy. The warrior leaves her tent, and without reservation, she delivers the best version of herself to the world.

Modern Solutions

Some people fear change. Others fear public speaking. Fear is the enemy of human progress. The strong warrior woman does everything in her power to become an effective leader. She listens to discussions about problems on the battlefield. She uses this information to analyze and develop strategies for advancement. She learns and practices excellent communication skills to publicly share the gift of ideas with her fellow woman. The warrior takes the road less traveled, and the path leads her to breakthrough.

Art And Humanity

Artistic individuals highly value the right to freedom of expression. The strong warrior woman recognizes that all humans are created with unique gifts and talents. People do not only have a right to act individually; they have a responsibility to do so. Creative ingenuity is a steel machine that clears a path to breakthrough. With this in mind, the warrior proceeds on the journey with an open heart and a ready mind. She nourishes her desire to constantly learn and grow, while also maintaining a fierce commitment to sharing her individuality with the world. As a result, humanity is well served by her existence.

Winning Pace

Life is sometimes referred to as a rat race. People become consumed with achieving a certain threshold of productivity, and the purpose becomes competing with and beating out the neighbor. The strong warrior woman works hard, but she takes time to smell the roses. People say, "She needs to hurry! She is wasting time!" The warrior pays no attention to these provocations. She knows that intense speed is not the key to arriving at her destination. She stays focused and never stops moving forward. Brilliant like the sun rising in the East and setting in the West, the warrior paces herself and completes her mission.

Her Secret Weapon

People claim with conviction, "She's a Renaissance woman!" The strong warrior woman is grateful for her facilities but she recognizes that a "Jill of all trades" is a master of none. She takes the time necessary to understand herself and the war she must wage. She analyzes the knowledge and experience necessary to claim victory. With this information at the forefront of her mind, she focuses on strengthening her most valuable device. The universe entrusted the warrior with many powers, but it is laser sharp training that makes her unstoppable in battle.

HARMONY OSWALD, ESQUIRE

Self-Help Wanted

Attempting to control the attitudes and actions of others can be a frustrating and fruitless endeavor. The only thing that a person can reliably manage is her own thoughts and behaviors. The strong warrior woman notices her companion repeatedly searching outside of herself for love, attention, and acceptance. She recognizes that this pursuit repeatedly ends in heartache, disappointment, and causes her fellow woman much grief. The warrior takes a different approach. She searches deep within herself to fulfill her own needs and desires. What the warrior finds is a high quality resource she can always rely upon.

Embrace Truth

People sometimes judge others based on preconceived notions about widely accepted, yet largely unchallenged, stereotypical behaviors. The strong warrior woman is committed to her own originality and authenticity. She is honest and transparent about whom she truly is. When a person learns something new about her that does not align well with traditionally established norms, they may become angry, surprised, or refuse to accept it. This does not unsettle or otherwise provoke the warrior. She believes it is better to be disliked for sharing her true self with the world than to be loved for acting fake.

Legend Of The Tombo

Some people fail to recognize the lasting repercussions of their actions. The strong warrior woman maintains an awareness that every move she makes echoes into eternity. She sets off to fulfill her mission with the speed, purpose, and agility of a dragonfly. Her energy vibrates far off into the distance, building up power as it travels along. In a drought-plagued region around the world, a farmer looks with anticipation toward the sky, as a lone raindrop cascades off her brim. "A storm is blowing in. It's a miracle!" she cries. The warrior uses her power for good, and her life impacts humanity in ways she will never know.

Don't Jump The Gun

Some warriors lose sleep because they feel unprepared for the voyage ahead. The strong warrior woman rests very well knowing that everything she needs for the current moment is right within her reach. She does not worry that she is not strong enough before she begins to climb mountains far off in the distance. She trusts that in proper time, the journey will provide her with the strength, stamina, and experience necessary to overcome every challenge the universe has predestined for her. The day of battle arrives, and the warrior is tenacious, bold, and ready for action.

HARMONY OSWALD, ESQUIRE

Filthy Rich

Stocks and mutual funds are a few ways to invest. The warrior wisely recognizes that the greatest investment she can ever make is in herself. She is committed to learning about the world she lives in and how she can make a positive difference. She becomes educated and knowledgeable regarding matters she cares deeply about. She hones her skills to become independent emotionally, physically, and financially. She treasures relationships with others but perceives them as a "special dessert," rather than the main course. The strong warrior woman is rich in both love and life because she invests in herself each day.

Moral Character

In society, some people are appalled by the thought of public defense lawyers representing perceived criminals. The strong warrior woman understands that these advocates protect the rights of potentially innocent citizens, to ensure the government does not jail people without due process. She also recognizes that attorneys who prosecute people accused of crimes also provide a valuable service in protecting the community. With this same approach, prior to choosing her own path, she considers ethical aspects of a variety of careers. The warrior ensures that her mission and purpose directly align with her values.

Propagate Love, Not War

The actions and attitudes a warrior delivers to her companions are reflected back to her with an enormous amount of accuracy. The strong warrior woman holds in highest regard her peacemaking mission. She refrains from causing physical, verbal, or any other type of harm to her fellow woman under any circumstance. The warrior understands that spreading love and kindness is her own divine gift to the universe, to humanity, and ultimately to herself.

Rainbow Filter

Everything seems to go wrong for certain members of the populace. These people never catch a break. They say, "We have no good opportunities! We are so unlucky!" The strong warrior woman views every situation through a rainbow filter. She uses her resourceful nature to make the most of her circumstances, connections, and abilities. Life provides all people with daily scenarios. Each situation can be perceived either as a curse of doom or an opportunity to progress. The warrior believes she is right where she belongs, and she decides she is lucky. She promptly returns to her mission of turning gravel into gold.

Security

The journey is filled with adventures, obstacles, and actors. Some travelers get lost and begin to rely on others to direct their course. The warrior prizes making her own decisions. She wisely recognizes that lifelong learning is a gateway to personal independence and financial freedom. She takes the time necessary to study herself and the world around her. Because she is clear about her own unique purpose, daily interactions with others do not confuse, intimidate, or deter her advancement. She is confident about who she is. The strong warrior woman knows what she is doing and where she is going.

Pioneer

When society establishes a "right" and "wrong" way to function or achieve results, opportunities for creative thinking fail to exist. The strong warrior woman views rigid attitudes as unproductive and limiting. She thrives in an innovative environment and perceives feeling vulnerable as a sign there is considerable potential to excel. She is not afraid of making an occasional mistake because she knows experimentation is both helpful and necessary in order to learn and grow. The warrior exudes and explores uncommon vision, and in return, it leads her to breakthrough.

HARMONY OSWALD, ESQUIRE

RDC Command (Review, Decide, Commit)

Impulsiveness can ruin relationships, lead to premature termination of prosperous business deals, and generally cause unnecessary mistakes. When time permits, it is always best to think things through rather than make a decision on the fly. The strong warrior woman consistently conducts herself with calculated precision. Prior to arriving at a solution to a problem, she takes the time necessary to learn about the facts. She asks questions to gather information. She remains open and alert to signs from the universe. After becoming fully informed, she makes her decision. Then, the warrior stands firm.

Glorious Reputation

Little splendor comes with vanquishing a weak opponent. The strong warrior woman gains her stalwart reputation from claiming victory after the most formidable duels. When she faces her fears to scale a mountain, fellow warriors exalt her and celebrate her immense courage. When she crosses a menacing divide, they admire her technique and respect her resolve. She is grounded, humble, and never seeks to impress. Glory chases down the warrior.

Inspire The Masses

Times get tough. Political and social turmoil cast a shadow of despair over the bravest of hearts. The strong warrior woman refrains from glancing in the direction of atrociousness, as she knows it will eventually turn her to stone. Instead, she continues to smile, persevere, take time to help her sister, and spread love to all of humanity. People say, "Why is she so happy? Doesn't she realize we are all doomed?" The warrior ignores these bleak innuendos, and continues to fight the good fight. Her zeal inspires people.

Code Of Discipline

If a woman thinks she can do something, she is right. If she lacks faith, she will never succeed. The strong warrior woman believes the sky is the limit. She refuses to conform her thinking to how things have "always been done" or other limiting attitudes that might taint her resolve to reach for the stars. She surrounds herself with messages of inspiration, hope, and courage. When a negative thought enters her mind, she immediately deflects it as an enemy to progress. She exercises control over her thoughts and actions. The warrior's success is a product of self-discipline.

HARMONY OSWALD, ESQUIRE

Equipment Maintenance

The human body is a machine that must be handled with care in order to function properly. Preventative maintenance guards against premature destruction from heart attacks, cancer, and other diseases that plague humanity. The strong warrior woman has been issued mighty armor to fight the good fight. Her body is her vehicle and it is her duty to treat it with honor, dignity, and respect. Without it, she cannot fulfill her mission. She avoids partaking in activities that harm her. She engages in regular maintenance and upkeep of her earthly vessel. The warrior engages in physical warfare.

Life And Death

Death is uncomfortable for some people to discuss, mystical for others to ponder, and inevitable for all. The strong warrior woman understands life is both precious and fleeting. She makes the most of her time on earth. She lives each day with passion and purpose. From time to time, she crosses the path of a fallen warrior. She shares a moment of silence in honor, recognition, and acceptance of the season. When the moment has passed, she rises up to continue peacefully on her way. The warrior approaches life and death with a sense of calm.

HARMONY OSWALD, ESQUIRE

Renewal

Tom says she has missed her calling. Dick says she chose the wrong field. Harry tells her to hurry up and just get started. The warrior smiles politely, thanks them for sharing, and continues about the important business of pursuing her purpose. In order to help her fellow woman, she cannot allow other people's opinions to drown out the whisper of her heart. The strong warrior woman knows that what the world needs now is authenticity and renewed energy, not manufactured ideas.

Love Works

In modern, organized societies, individuals become knowledgeable in certain fields and then exchange related products or services for currency. When people specialize and trade, it provides a means of survival while creating economic efficiency. The strong warrior woman chooses her career path not to merely survive, but also to serve her fellow woman. She takes the time necessary to understand and develop her greatest skills and talents. She is committed to making a positive difference through her labor. The warrior views work as an extraordinary opportunity to share gifts of love with the world.

Wisdom From The Fray

"I will never change my point of view!" a close-minded individual asserts. What a person believes, however, is merely an attitude she adopted within the confines of past information. The strong warrior woman realizes that every new situation presents opportunities for learning. The key is to open her mind and listen to truly understand the person presenting information. Some of the things stated may not resonate with her soul, but in every circumstance there is a takeaway gift if she is willing to receive it. She adjusts her outlook periodically as she grows and matures in battle. The warrior gathers wisdom from the fray.

Simple Joys

Life can get complicated. There's work to do, bills to pay, errands to run, and the list goes on. When an unplanned item arises, such as a car in need of repair, it can begin to feel like the day itself will surely implode. The strong warrior woman knows how busy life can be. She is well aware of the treacherous war being waged for her attention. She is careful and particularized in deciding how she will spend her valuable time. She is willing to say "no" when appropriate and necessary. The warrior strives for simplicity.

HARMONY OSWALD, ESQUIRE

Unruffled

At times, chaos is inescapable. Peace is nowhere to be found. The strong warrior woman refuses to allow disarray to kill her positive vibe. When pandemonium erupts, she releases all expectations and fully accepts the present moment as it is. She approaches the circumstance with an open heart and mind. She searches for harmony in the midst of turmoil, and she finds it waiting patiently for her. The warrior breathes freely as a ray of sunshine peeks out from behind the clouds to shine light and love upon her individual path to breakthrough.

Team World

The most intelligent and strategic of warriors sometimes makes the mistake of trying to do everything solo. This choice is both limiting and exhausting. The strong warrior woman observes the far-reaching benefits of teamwork. She recognizes that diversity of thought and action intensifies and extends progress beyond the scope of what is possible when working alone. She never acts too swiftly without first granting her team an opportunity to contribute as well. The warrior is a woman of the world. Where she ventures, the planet ventures with her.

For The Love Of Battle

The strong warrior woman notices people all around her who have lost their faith. They express hopelessness. Their days are filled with agony and distress. The warrior does everything in her power to maintain a positive outlook. She clings to her own vision of a high quality future filled with many worthwhile possibilities. Plus, she believes in the goodness and potential of her fellow woman. She always makes sure her rucksack contains faith and hope, but she only marches forward when her heart is filled with love. If love is present, the warrior knows she is ready to fight the good fight.

Eradicate Stereotypes

Unconscious bias plagues society. Some individuals think black men are criminals. Others believe women are untrustworthy. Harmful stereotypes like these apply to race, gender, sexuality, age, and the list goes on. The strong warrior woman recognizes that she enjoys privilege in some areas of her life while in others she is part of a group historically discriminated against. She exercises a present state of awareness. She listens to personal stories of the individuals she meets. The warrior is tolerant, inclusive, and never forms opinions based on unexamined assumptions.

Five Star Standards

An old adage advises people not to worry about the little things in life. The strong warrior woman does recognize the benefit of "picking her battles," but she also knows sometimes the "devil is in the details." She often chooses to overlook small discrepancies so that when an occasional issue arises which she decides to discuss with her companions, they realize it is very important. When it comes to implementing her own daily tasks, however, she always pays close attention to details. The warrior holds herself to the highest standards of excellence.

Keep It Real

In today's world, some people maintain a public persona that is quite different than their true identity. They showcase the highlights while hiding the hardships. The strong warrior woman does not spend her precious time being fake. She does not rely on false friendships or "likes" to build her ego. She lives her life with authenticity, integrity, and confidence. People trust her because she keeps it real. In the case of the warrior, what you see is actually what you get.

Prepare To Conquer

Making a decision requires striking a balance between careful contemplation and accepting risk. The strong warrior woman notices people becoming so frightened by the possibility of making a mistake that they are unable to choose in a timely manner. When a window of opportunity opens, a person must act swiftly, or the window will close, and they will miss the opportunity. When the warrior's preparation meets a chance from above, she quickly and purposefully acts. Magic occurs. "She is so lucky!" people shout. The warrior is prepared and confident. When she takes a risk, the stars align to help her.

Social Justice

The strong warrior woman cares about respect, tolerance, and inclusion for all. She believes it is important to help others succeed. One day, she hears someone shout, "Why should we help people who are different from us?" Another person adds, "Lets keep things the same as they've always been. Even if it doesn't work for everyone, at least we are used to it." This disappoints the warrior, but she decides not to take it personally. She wisely recognizes that such people are not her opponents. They are opponents of social justice. In the end, justice will be served.

HARMONY OSWALD, ESQUIRE

March Along The High Road

No matter how much a warrior strives for peace, periodically, conflict will ensue. Living in a world full of diverse people means disagreements will arise. The warrior accepts conflict as part of the job description, but she refuses to allow a little dissonance to get in the way of completing her mission. She exercises mindfulness to continuously reside at a higher plane of consciousness. Chaos and disarray have zero power over her. The strong warrior woman chooses to march along the high road, and the path leads her to breakthrough.

Eccentric Treasures

When large masses of people make automatic, unexamined choices to conform to societal standards, it is referred to as groupthink. The strong warrior woman recognizes that this type of decision-making can lead to dysfunction. Diversity of thought is a key factor for efficient productivity and human advancement. For this reason, she commits to her own originality while considering other perspectives as well. She is clear about her mission and presses forward, in spite of critics who do not understand her plan. A warrior who is ahead of her time is sometimes misunderstood.

Hers To Win

"I can't do this! It's too hard!" are slogans of quitters.

The strong warrior woman believes she can do anything

she wants to do, as long as she perseveres through

hardships and does her best. When things become very

difficult and she begins to doubt her abilities, she

remembers the wisdom shared by strong and brave fighters

of the past. Even if she does not always succeed, a warrior

does not fail when she loses, she only fails when she quits.

Understanding this truth, she proceeds to breakthrough.

The universe never gives a warrior fighting the good fight

any more than she can handle.

Cosmic Choices

Each day, people make thousands of decisions that specifically determine the quality and characteristics of the future. The strong warrior woman embraces every opportunity to select well because she knows that what she picks is literally what she gets. Before arriving at a high stakes resolution that will greatly impact her life, she takes time to research and analyze the best possible options and outcomes. The warrior makes choices that are out of this world, and as a result, she shines like a star in the heavens!

Bold Advocacy

From the sidelines, people can relax and enjoy the view. Watching others make their moves may be safer and easier, but it requires giving up all power to impact strategies and outcomes. The strong warrior woman has a big heart for the issues she cares about. She understands the importance of rising up to fight for a cause. She knows that oppression thrives where people remain still and silent. When she desires change, she is no coward. The warrior boldly protests injustice, and her fellow woman makes no mistake about where she stands.

Heroic Valor And Mighty Fortitude

The most amazing books feature a heroine engaging in tales of passion, feats of rescue, or wild adventures. The strong warrior woman's own days on earth create a storyline consisting of love, loss, commitment, brokenness, treachery, courage, and boldly advocating for the principles she believes in. When she looks in the mirror, she sees the reflection of a fighter marked with glorious lines and scars of battle - including a few that slipped through her hands. She continues to fight the good fight. She perseveres when times get tough. The warrior is the hero of her own story.

Deflect Negative Energy

One way to quickly throw away power is to explain the reason for an action to someone who is not an allied force. This type of behavior legitimizes doubt and does little to convince a critic to become a fan. The warrior notices that the companions within her tent do not require her to provide further details. Plus, she suspects that the enemies of her life have no intention of understanding her. She is confident in her mission. The strong warrior woman never explains and never apologizes for fighting the good fight.

Revelations

Some people travel with their eyes shut. They don't literally keep them closed, but they might as well. Their world is gray because their mind has distracted them from the pristine beauty of the present moment. The strong warrior woman knows that in order to maintain an accurate perception of her immediate surroundings, she must stay present, mindful, and alert. The warrior travels with her eyes wide open. The universe delivers signs to guide and protect her.

The Warrior Has Arrived

Anyone who has ever taken a long trip with a small child knows that a kid can be impatient to get to the final destination. "Are we there yet?" they ask, anxiously anticipating the fabulous place they expect to arrive at down the road. The strong warrior woman holds a clear vision for her future and perseveres to meet her goals. In the meantime, she holds the perspective that she has already arrived. She takes time each day to celebrate her progress. The warrior wisely recognizes that the gift is in the journey.

Steady Leadership

Reactive responses that are sparked by rage tend to ruin relationships and spawn regret. The strong warrior woman practices maintaining a present state of awareness. She conducts herself in a grounded, alert manner. When her companion approaches her with a problem, she listens closely. She asks questions and takes the time necessary to fully understand the issue before her. She is approachable, even-tempered, and steadfast. She delivers a thoughtful answer when the time is right. She acts with patience and purpose. The warrior is a leader among her peers.

Send It Upward

Many benefits arise from trusting a higher power. The strong warrior woman fully embraces this truth. Rather than attempting to control that which is not within her sphere of influence, she gives the universe permission to act on her behalf. She meditates in prayerful contemplation, sending positive energy into the heavens. Then, she relaxes and enjoys the day. She is on an important mission. The warrior does not waste precious energy trying to manage things not within her scope of control.

Win The War

Upon losing a battle, some people feel completely defeated. They surrender prematurely. The warrior wisely recognizes it is not a single battle that counts. What matters is winning the war. She constantly focuses on long-term goals and strategies. She embraces every opportunity to improve herself. She knows the champion is often times not the fastest or smartest on the battlefield. The one who triumphs is she who presses forward with fierce determination, unwavering persistence, and remarkable courage. The strong warrior woman may lose a single battle, but ultimately it is she who wins the war.

Sparkle

Unshared talents, like unopened gifts, are useless and wasteful. The strong warrior woman understands that fighting the good fight requires dedication to the mission of spreading kindness, hope, and love to all of humanity. She approaches this duty with gratitude, eagerness, positivity, and a lavish love for her fellow woman. Her life resembles that of a billion dollar lottery winner sharing her fortune with an abundance of friends. She gives of herself freely and with a joyful heart. The warrior's star shines brightly!

The Legend Of Her

Life gets extremely busy. Some people never take a moment to stop and reflect upon their purpose, as they go through the same motions day after day. "This is all just a waste of time," they report. The strong warrior woman refuses to live a life filled with meaningless mediocrity. She invests in herself. She takes the time necessary to understand her unique gifts, the issues she cares about, and how she can make a difference for her fellow woman. With power and conviction, she embraces her whole purpose. The warrior makes it count because she is legendary.

HARMONY OSWALD, ESQUIRE

War Hero

There are moments when every warrior doubts herself. At times, the strong warrior woman questions her will to fight. When this occurs, she takes a moment to quietly reflect. She invites the forces of the universe to guide and protect her. She remains open to all that she might become.

At once, truth shines brightly upon her like the noonday sun. It reminds her that she is strong, courageous, and determined to fight the good fight. With humble gratitude, she accepts this gift of enlightenment. She rises to the occasion. The warrior is a force to be reckoned with. She is a war hero.

Reinventing Fabulous

Getting older is cause for celebration. Every year lived is a gift, and every new day is an opportunity to progress. The strong warrior woman has traveled a great distance. She looks to the past and sees where she has been. She won some battles and lost a few, but more importantly, she learned invaluable lessons along the way. She looks to the future to see where she is going. She plans to pursue her goals with passion and conviction, to make a positive impact in the world. She looks at where she is today, and she is grateful for the woman she has become. The warrior is phenomenal, and she is constantly getting better.

Declare The Winner

Focusing on scarcity and lack is a surefire pathway to doom. The strong warrior woman never compares herself to others. She chose her own path, and she does not complain when things get difficult or setbacks arise. She realizes hardships come with the territory of fighting the good fight, and she recognizes the prize is in the progress. The warrior focuses on cultivating the traits she possesses that will help her to become a champion. Luck is on her side, because she declares herself a winner.

Shine On

There is little benefit in striving for normalcy. The strong warrior woman believes every human is uniquely gifted and highly valuable. She fully embraces her talents and commits to sharing the best version of herself with the world. When she seeks encouragement, she looks to female leaders such as Oprah Winfrey, Mother Theresa, and Madonna, who have lived their lives independently, authentically, and powerfully. The warrior is a star in her own right. She shines brightly during this moment in space and time.

HARMONY OSWALD, ESQUIRE

110% All In

As the journey comes to a close, people tend to look back at life, thinking of quality moments and analyzing regrets. Many times, they wish they had listened to the quiet whisper of their hearts. The warrior honors her future by making wise choices today. She listens to her better angel as it implores her to live each day with zest and fervor. She approaches the journey with a heart full of love, a commitment to excellence, and a passion for celebration. At day's end, she is at peace. The strong warrior woman went all in.

Forward March

When traveling through small villages, the strong warrior woman meets people who speak of dreams from the past. When they were younger, they felt excited about the adventures life had in store. As they grew older, people began to pressure them to remain in the village. "It's not safe on the outside! It's too risky. It won't work!" The villager's stories remind her that pursuing a vision requires great courage. It sometimes becomes necessary to shed an old identity to grow fiercer in battle. With a soft heart, she thanks her newfound friends for the gifts they so graciously shared. The warrior must now be on her way.

HARMONY OSWALD, ESQUIRE

She sheds her old identity

to become fiercer in battle.

The warrior must now be on her way.

About the Author

Harmony Oswald, Esq. is the Founder and Managing Attorney at Parazim, where the mission is to elevate and champion the most effective, extraordinary, and powerful women in the world. In Silicon Valley and beyond, Parazim is best known for its **#breakthroughhabitude** of women helping women. Visit www.parazim.com to learn more.

Ms. Oswald is a native of Western Pennsylvania. Her time as a journalist led to travels from Europe to California, where countless strong and talented women influenced her journey.

She is a Veteran of the U.S. Army, where she served two years in Wuerzburg, Germany with the 1st Infantry Division. She was honored to receive the Army Achievement Medal for her service as a soldier and broadcast journalist overseas.

She earned her Juris Doctor degree at Santa Clara University School of Law where she received a High Tech Law Certificate, with Honors, and a High Tech Excellence Award. She was selected for a High Tech Internship at Google where she wrote a defensive patent publication, published by Google. She received the Witkin Award for her research and writing on Gender and the Law issues. Ms. Oswald also holds a B.A. in Law and Society from Penn State University where she graduated summa cum laude, and an Associate Degree from The Art Institute (Bradley Academy).

Ms. Oswald competed on NBC's Fear Factor, where she unlocked herself from a platform dangling from a helicopter and jumped into a lake, in a timed setting. Her breakthrough partner and husband is Rick and she is blessed with two amazing kids, Tenor and Sterling.

Photo credits and special thanks to

www.elliehonlphotography.com

Design credits and special thanks to

www.peggiejeanie.com

THE SOCIAL JUSTICE ART GALLERY

www.zimcreate.com

At Zim Create, we unleash the power of creativity to elevate and champion the most effective, extraordinary, and powerful women in the world. All of the fine artwork available at our online gallery is created by female artists, and a portion of every sale goes toward advancing female artists, entrepreneurs, and women running for office.

New Artists
Zim Create loves meeting talented new artists! If you would like the opportunity to sell your art while also helping to make a positive impact in the world, visit Zim Create and review our Artist Guide to learn more.

Impact Investing
We offer the unique opportunity to purchase superb quality artwork from established and emerging female artists who exude amazing potential for their art to rise in value over time. Our collectors can feel confident knowing that every purchase at Zim Create is a wise investment, in more ways than one. Support a Parazim Breakthrough. Purchase art today!

Thanks for being a champion for women and girls.
YOU ARE A HERO!

Made in the USA
San Bernardino, CA
29 April 2017